Squid Twins

by Rick Trevia • illustrated by Niki Leonidou

It is spring. The squid twins get set for school.

Splat and Sprat splash.

"Not too much," says Mom.

"This mat is wet."

Splat and Sprat squish.

"Not too fast," says Dad.

"It is slick."

Splat and Sprat help Mom.

"Good lunches help squids get

strong," says Mom.

Splat and Sprat get snacks from Dad.

"Put snacks in your boxes."

The twins get their backpacks.

Splat's strap has split. Mom fixes it.

When the bus gets there,
Splat and Sprat get kisses.
Then Splat and Sprat run.